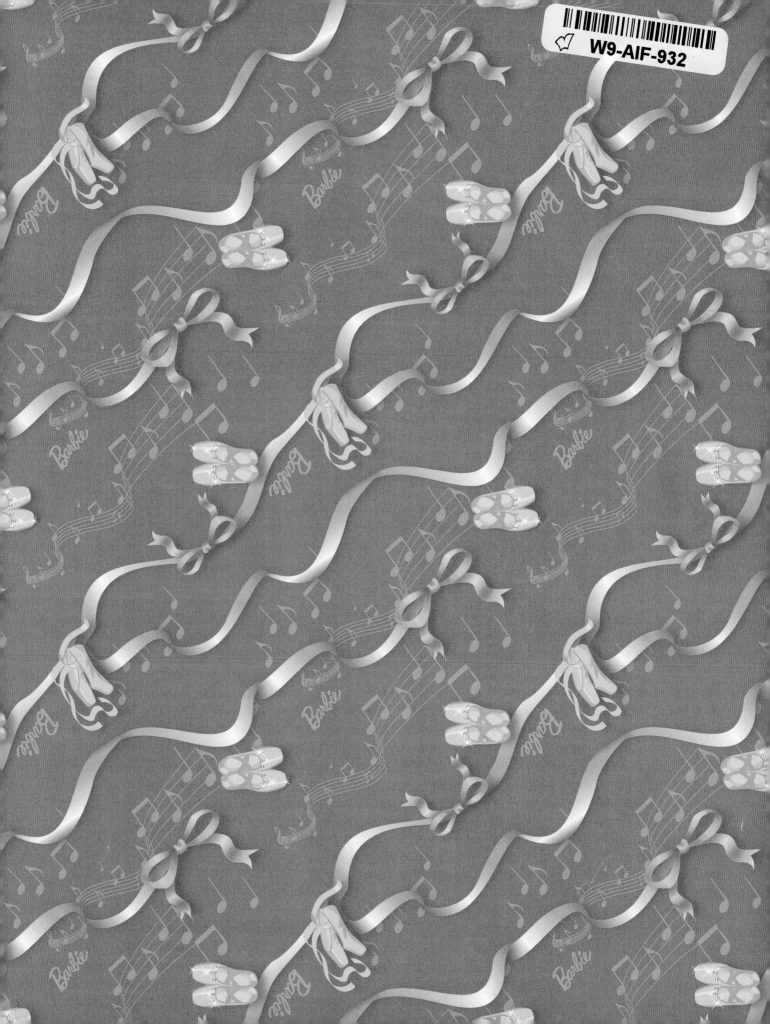

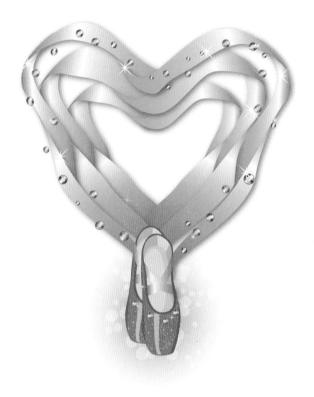

Special thanks to Diane Reichenberger, Cindy Ledermann, Ann McNeill, Kim Culmone, Emily Kelly, Sharon Woloszyk, Carla Alford, Rita Lichtwardt, Kathy Berry, Rob Hudnut, David Wiebe, Shelley Dvi-Vardhana, Gabrielle Miles, Technicolor, and Walter P. Martishius

ISBN: 978-0-307-98167-7
Printed in the United States of America
10 9 8 7 6 5 4 3 2

Adapted by Kristen L. Depken
Based on the screenplay by Alison Taylor
Illustrated by Ulkutay Design Group

 A GOLDEN BOOK • NEW YORK

One day, at a popular ballet academy, a dance student named Kristyn watched beautiful dancers glide and twirl across the stage.

The young dancer stared in amazement as Tara, the school's talented star ballerina, rehearsed with a handsome dancer named Dillon. Kristyn knew every ballet by heart and dreamed of becoming the prima ballerina.

"I wish I could dance like that," said Kristyn with a sigh. "She looks like a star!" Kristyn had a smaller part in the school's upcoming recital.

"Let's have the milkmaid number!" called Madame Natasha, the strict instructor.

Kristyn took the stage and began to dance her part with precision. Madame Natasha was pleased, until Kristyn began to stray from the choreography.

"Stop!" cried Madame Natasha.

Startled out of her dream dance, Kristyn fell and ripped her shoe.

"I've seen other girls try to dance their own ideas, and I promise you, that story does not end well," warned Madame Natasha. "Now, please get yourself some new shoes. Take five, everyone!"

Kristyn followed her friend Hailey to the costume shop to get a new pair of dance shoes. Hailey was the assistant to the head costume designer, Madame Katerina.

Kristyn picked up a beautiful blue dress. It was from the ballet *Giselle*. "I wish I could dance the lead in *Giselle*, or just once be Odette, the queen of the swans in *Swan Lake*," she said.

Hailey emerged from the shoe closet. "Plenty of shoes, Madame," she said. "But no size fives."

"Wait," said Madame Katerina. "I might have something here." She went to a high shelf and pulled down a pair of bright pink toe shoes. "They're for you, my dear," she said, and handed them to Kristyn.

"They're beautiful!" Kristyn exclaimed. She sat down on a bench and slipped them on. Then she took Hailey's hand and stood up again.

Suddenly, Kristyn's pink shoes began to sparkle. She watched in amazement as her dress shimmered, and then began to magically transform from a simple pink practice outfit to the beautiful blue *Giselle* dress. Her long blond hair changed to a strawberry blond color and was swept into a classic updo.

Meanwhile, the costume shop glittered magically and then faded away. It was slowly replaced by a lush fairy-tale forest.

"*Whoa!*" said Kristyn and Hailey at the same time.

Before the girls knew what was happening, they heard music.
Kristyn and Hailey hurried down the forest path to a field
surrounded by cottages. A group of villagers stepped onto
the field and began to dance a scene from the ballet *Giselle*.

Kristyn and Hailey suddenly realized that Kristyn *was* Giselle! The pink shoes had transformed her!

"Dance now, ask questions later!" said Hailey, pushing Kristyn toward the center of the field. Kristyn danced the role of Giselle flawlessly.

"I love these shoes!" she squealed.

When she had finished dancing, Kristyn was approached by
two young men. The first was a nobleman named Albrecht, who
desperately wanted to marry Giselle.

The second young man was a peasant named Hilarion. "Giselle
and I are to be married tomorrow," he insisted.

As Albrecht and Hilarion began to argue over Kristyn, Hailey
pulled her aside. "We've got to get out of here!" she said.

The girls ran into the woods and hurried down the forest path. They hid behind a tree just as an icy sleigh glided past them. A woman with a cold stare and a majestic blue gown stepped down and approached Albrecht and Hilarion.

"The Snow Queen!" Kristyn whispered nervously.

When the Snow Queen saw that the ballet was not proceeding as usual, she demanded to see Giselle.

"Find her and bring her to me," ordered the Snow Queen. "I will *not* tolerate this kind of disruption. The ballet must be perfect."

The friends were venturing deep into the woods when Hailey
had an idea. "The shoes!" she exclaimed. "You put on the shoes
and *poof!*—we're here in wacky land. So if you take them off . . ."

"I'm not taking off these shoes!" cried Kristyn. They had
helped her to dance like she had never danced before, and she
wasn't ready to stop. Kristyn darted into a thicket of trees and
soon found herself at the edge of a shimmering lake.

When she saw her reflection in the crystal clear water, Kristyn gasped. Her dress had transformed into a beautiful purple-and-white feathered tutu, and her hair was now chestnut brown.

A group of swans swam to the distant shore, then turned into graceful ballet dancers.

Kristyn and Hailey were in the ballet *Swan Lake*!

The dancers approached Kristyn and crowned her Odette,
the Swan Queen from *Swan Lake*. Kristyn was delighted.
   "Kristyn, we can't get involved here," said Hailey
nervously. "Let's go."

Just then, a handsome young man introduced himself. "My name is Prince Siegfried," he said. Siegfried took Kristyn's hand and asked her to dance, thinking she was the Swan Queen, Odette.

Kristyn danced from her heart, and the prince was charmed. "I want to invite you to a ball tonight at the royal pavilion," Siegfried said. "Please say you'll come."

"I'll be there," replied Kristyn.

After Prince Siegfried left, a man in a dark cloak appeared.
"Rothbart!" exclaimed Kristyn and Hailey. They instantly
recognized the evil magician from *Swan Lake*.

Rothbart raised both arms and directed a spell at Kristyn
and Hailey, turning both girls into swans!

"My daughter, Odile, will marry Prince Siegfried," he cackled
as he magically transformed his daughter into Odette the Swan
Queen. Rothbart tried to capture both girls, but they escaped
into the water before he could reach them.

"There's only one place we can go," said Kristyn. "To the ball!"
Only Siegfried's love could break Rothbart's spell. If Kristyn didn't
get to the prince in time, she and Hailey would be human only
when the sun was down. Every time the sun rose, they would turn
into swans again.

"It's going to be a long walk with these tiny feet," said Hailey.

"We've got these!" exclaimed Kristyn, flapping her swan wings.
Soon both girls were flying toward the palace.

When they arrived at the ball, Kristyn and Hailey discovered that Rothbart had changed his daughter, Odile, to make her look like Odette the Swan Queen. If Kristyn didn't stop Siegfried from falling in love with Odile, Rothbart's swan spell would be permanent.

Kristyn and Hailey watched helplessly as Rothbart introduced his daughter to Prince Siegfried and his mother.

"Shall we dance?" the prince asked a smiling Odile.

"We've got to stop those two!" cried Kristyn.

Kristyn and Hailey burst into the ballroom just in time to interrupt Odile's dance with Prince Siegfried. They flew around the room, honking and flapping their wings. As the sun went down, Kristyn was magically changed back into Odette. A moment later, Hailey became human again, too.

Kristyn began to dance. She spun and twirled gracefully across the dance floor as Odile looked on with jealousy. "This is *my* dance," Odile hissed angrily.

The prince looked from one girl to the other, not sure which one was his true love. But as Kristyn continued to dance, he became more certain.

The prince took Kristyn's hand, and they danced beautifully together. "This isn't how it goes!" cried Odile in frustration.

But Siegfried didn't hear her. He was in love with Kristyn. The spell had been broken.

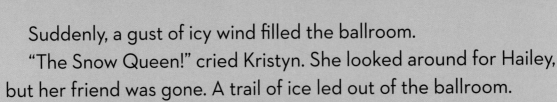

Suddenly, a gust of icy wind filled the ballroom.

"The Snow Queen!" cried Kristyn. She looked around for Hailey, but her friend was gone. A trail of ice led out of the ballroom.

Kristyn had to save Hailey. "I'm sorry, but I have to go!" she told Siegfried. As she raced out of the pavilion and followed the trail of ice, she ran into Albrecht and Hilarion.

"Please take me to the Snow Queen's palace," she said. "I have to get my friend back!"

Albrecht and Hilarion agreed to help. Together the three set out for the frozen palace.

When Kristyn and the young men reached the palace, they found the Snow Queen in a huge, icy throne room. Hailey was trapped in a block of ice.

"So you're the one who's changing the ballet stories," snarled the Snow Queen when she saw Kristyn. "Giselle? Or might I say Odette?"

The Snow Queen raised her arms and moved them as if she were a puppeteer, making Kristyn pirouette uncontrollably.

Spinning faster and faster, Kristyn closed
her eyes and began to dance across the throne
room in her own style. As she leaped and twirled
gracefully, her outfit changed to a blush-rose
pink, and her hair returned to its natural blond
color. Kristyn was herself again!

"No!" cried the Snow Queen. "There's only one way to tell this story!"

"There is more than one way to tell *my* story," replied Kristyn.

Suddenly, magical rays of light shone through the palace, and the Snow Queen disappeared.

Kristyn rushed to Hailey and helped her up. "Everything's okay now," Kristyn said. "It's time to go."

The friends shared a happy hug. Then Kristyn unlaced the pink shoes and took them off.

The ballet world grew hazy, and soon both girls were back at the ballet academy.

"Kristyn, it's your turn for the recital!" Madame Katerina cried. There were ballet scouts in the audience who would be choosing dancers for an international ballet production.

Tara stepped forward and handed Kristyn a new pair of ballet shoes. Hailey quickly finished Kristyn's costume just in time for her performance.

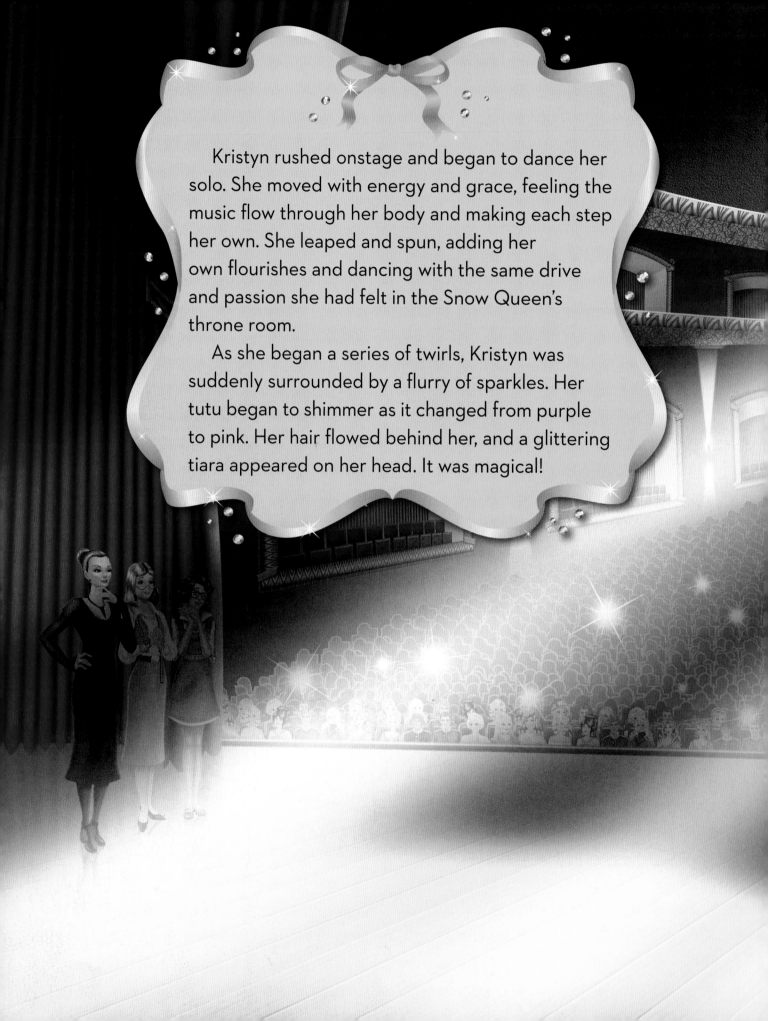

Kristyn rushed onstage and began to dance her solo. She moved with energy and grace, feeling the music flow through her body and making each step her own. She leaped and spun, adding her own flourishes and dancing with the same drive and passion she had felt in the Snow Queen's throne room.

As she began a series of twirls, Kristyn was suddenly surrounded by a flurry of sparkles. Her tutu began to shimmer as it changed from purple to pink. Her hair flowed behind her, and a glittering tiara appeared on her head. It was magical!

When Kristyn finished, the audience burst into applause.
Hailey rushed onstage and wrapped Kristyn in a huge hug.
"Nicely done, Kristyn," said Tara with a smile.
The ballet scouts chose Tara as the lead in the performance
of *Giselle*.
Then one of the scouts said, "I've been planning a new
ballet, and I want to build it around Kristyn and her ideas."
Kristyn couldn't believe it! She might not dance like Tara, but
she danced from her heart—and that was what mattered most.

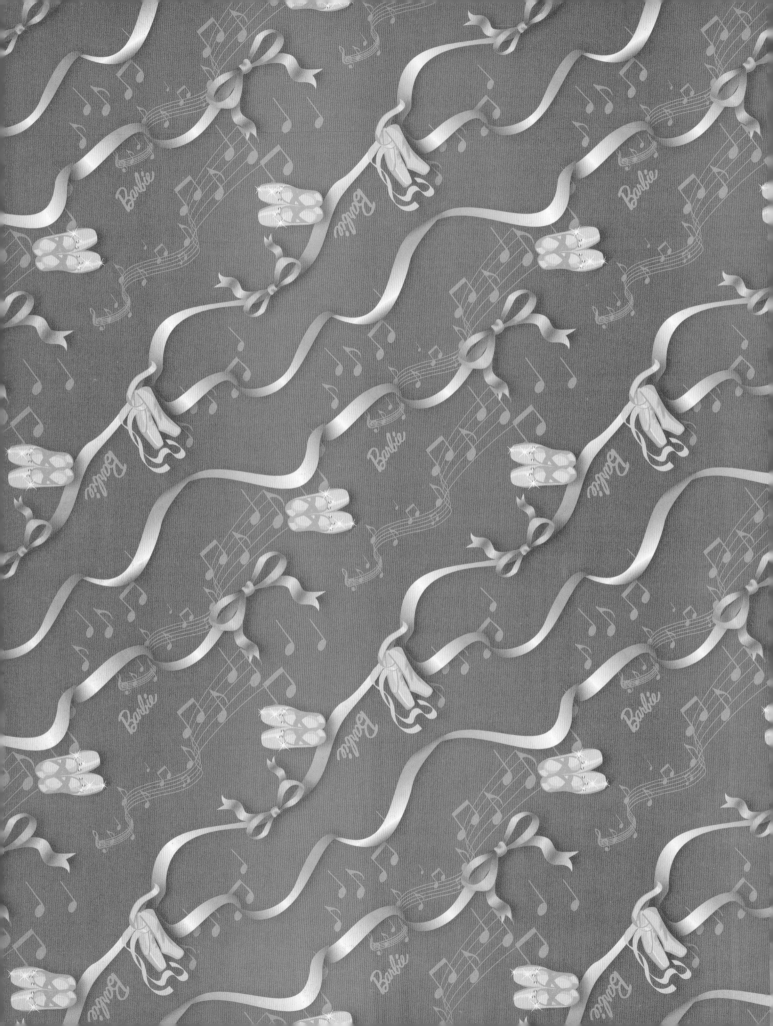